The Spotted Unicorn

Written and illustrated by Marilyn Hoobler

Mare's Field Publishing
9 Warrenton Drive
Silver Spring, Maryland 20904
©2010 All rights reserved.

No part of this book may be reproduced, stored in a retrieval system, or transmitted by any means without the written permission of the author.

First published by Mare's Field Publishing, August 2010
ISBN: 978-0-9822066-1-4
Printed in the United States of America
LaVergne, Tennessee U.S.A. 37086

for my children

Long ago, in a dark forest, there lived a unicorn. Other unicorns were all white, but he had large brown spots. Also, his hooves were three different colors, and two swirled stripes marred his horn. He lived happily alone and had no desire to leave the forest.

One year, as summer's bright days yielded to autumn, that changed. The crisp air had pinched the lifeblood from the leaves and they, blazing in brilliant hues, prepared to die. Evening fell and the unicorn lay sleeping. He had spent the day leaping and romping in the forest, rejoicing in its beauty, and now, he began to dream. The leaves stood strangely silent. The moon shone through

some lower branches, which had been the first to drop their foliage. Frosty puffs of air fluttered from the unicorn's nostrils. A breeze ruffled the hair on his back. The breezed stiffened and the leaves, leaving their silence, stirred into a melodious roar. Startled, he awoke. Blinking, he stared wildly at the canopy waving above him. As the trees danced before the moonlight, he could see in flashes of light his mottled form. At first he thought nothing of it, but then, to his surprise, the wind gathered into a whirlwind, which, driving upward, stripped more and more leaves off the trees. As they spiraled up, the moon quickened its gaze on the beast. He trembled at the violence of the night. Miserable and alone, he felt cold and afraid. He had always thought it silly and weak that other unicorns sought comforts and palaces, but now, for the first time, he longed for them. He wanted to meet a princess.

He must find a castle and seek the princess inside. As he imagined himself entering the gates, a terrible truth came home to him: He would be repellant to any true princess. Wide awake, he trudged through the forest, thinking of every possible way to rid himself of his spots.

Could they be rolled out? He looked for a clearing and, when he came upon one, tried rolling them out.

Could they be washed out? After hours of wandering, he came to a pond deep enough to swim in. But the spots glistened darkly as he climbed out of the pond.

Could he scrape them off on a tree? He

wandered farther until he found one he knew of with very rough bark. The spots remained, now stinging.

He wandered all night. He no longer knew the way back to the nice little hollow he had lived in. He left the protective shelter of the forest.

As the sun rose, it brightened his irregularities. He hid under a tall spruce tree and fell asleep.

In the merciful darkness, he awoke and set out again, with nothing to do but hope that somewhere in the world there was a princess who would want him.

At night he looked up at the pure white sphere of the moon. "If only I could have your color."

When winter came, a gentle breeze blew up early one morning as he slept. It strengthened into a stiff blast. Still the unicorn slept. Each frosty breath from his nostrils sent puffs into the air as downy flakes swirled around him.

When he opened his eyes, he dared not move. He could feel the snow covering every inch of his body and for the first time in his life he was glistening with pure white brilliance. The sun sparkled on his wintry gown.

"This must be what it feels like!" He remained perfectly still.

But the sun grew warmer and melted the snow away. He was cold and wet. And still spotted.

When the wind blew cold again, the unicorn walked to keep warm. Each blast was more terrible than the one before, and the unicorn staggered. Night fell. The storm did not abate, and the world was a blur of white snow. On he struggled.

By the break of day, his legs had numbed past feeling. His joints burned like firebrands, and his mind sickened with exhaustion. His body began to tremble. Finally the unicorn collapsed.

Just ahead of him, though he could not see it through the snow, a stone wall rose up. In its center was an iron gate with slender bars under a picture of a perfectly white unicorn with a scarlet ribbon around its neck. Face down on the ground inside the gate lay a young girl. Her father knelt beside her. The two peered into a pool, which, despite the fierce storm, had not frozen. The moon's reflection faded on the surface of the pool as the sky paled.

The girl blew on the surface of the water causing ripples to form. An evergreen tree grew near the pool and occasionally she reached up to shake an overhanging bough and release its cover of snow. The flurries fell into the water and disappeared, to her delight.

"Do you want me to blow harder?" she asked her father.

"No, you've blown just right for now." He stood to brush the snow from his clothes.

"And there he is!" He was looking through the gate at the half-frozen animal.

"Is it my own?" she asked.

"Put your royal cloak over him and we'll bring him in," said the king (for he was a king).

Fatigue had yielded to the unicorn its finest gift:

He slept peacefully even as the girl wrapped him in her wool cloak of curly lambskin and as the father picked him up. Together they carried him, the girl supporting his head and minding the horn.

When the unicorn awoke, he found himself in the warm confines of a palace and surrounded

by servants. Best of all, a young girl held his head in her lap and fed him rose petals. Only a princess could have rose petals in the winter.

"Now then"—it was her father speaking—"You know the rules. During the day you may cover him with your cloak and bring him inside, but at night he must remain in the courtyard.

"Why can't I stay inside?" the unicorn asked her later (for unicorns can talk to princesses).

"You're not white, you silly!" Then came the peals of laughter that he would come to love.

The princess was kind. She lent him a light in the evening, so he would not be afraid in the dark courtyard, and also her royal cloak.

The light of the moon, too, helped him through the long nights. But sometimes,

before the break of day, the unicorn fretted. He tried rolling in the snow to whiten his spots. He scraped against the iron bars of the gate, especially where they had rusted.

One night he dropped the cloak and plunged into the magic pool (for the pool was magic) with a noisy splash, but he almost drowned. He had planned to jump right out, but the pool turned out to be very deep and he began to sink. At that moment he heard a crash that sounded like thunder. It was the palace door banging open. The princess had to run out in her dressing gown. Plunging into the icy depths she grabbed his mane and swam to the top. They stood, drenched and shivering.

"It is dangerous in there!" she said. "You don't understand. There is evil there that would harm you—snakes that want to hurt you." Covering him with the cloak, she returned to the palace.

Soon enough, the unicorn realized he could not remove the spots. Yet he could not resist the thought that perhaps this time he would succeed. Herein lies the sad and repeated tale of failure when folly is allowed to triumph over wisdom. Fortunately, terror now fenced the magic pool and in this small way the simple beast had made his first step toward becoming wise.

In most respects, unicorns are not wise. They do understand magic, which is different from wisdom. If, however, a unicorn is fortunate enough to find a princess who is herself wise, he will begin to be educated, just as all those who are around her. This princess was as wise as she was good. The unicorn came to her when she was still quite young, and as she grew, he also grew in the wisdom that was hers.

Thus it dawned on his little mind (for little it was) that there actually was some manner of cure for his condition of spots. The means of it, however, eluded him. He often asked, but the princess only laughed with a certain twinkle in her eye. He knew he would never get the information except in her own time.

By listening to the servants, he determined that the secret had something to do with the sun, a full moon, the magic pool, and the wool cloak. At last, when he almost gave way to despair, his mistress revealed the secret.

It was in the dead of winter. She had awakened him early, just at dawn, and together they left the palace. Winding through a wood nearby, they came to an inlet of water that stretched endlessly ahead. This was not the first time the unicorn had seen it. They had passed it before. The sandy beach lay situated somewhere between the palace to the right and a pinnacle of land far to the left. Previously the unicorn had seen what appeared to be a small boulder far out into the water, but this morning the low tide revealed a rocky path that went clear through to the stone, now in full view. Unveiled, it proved to be of astonishing size.

"Come." The princess walked out onto the path. The rock proved easy to climb, and once on top, the land and water lay in a breathtaking panorama around them.

"Do you see that city?" the princess asked, gesturing toward the pinnacle of land.

"Yes."

"That and all you see is mine."

She looked at him.

"Yes?"

"More that you cannot see is also mine. It is all mine by right."

The unicorn looked toward the pinnacle. The sun had just begun its ascent. The lights of the city twinkled faintly, and the sky swam in pale colors of yellow, orange, and blue—a blue that he, for the first time, noticed perfectly matched the princess's silk gown. The waters of the low tide oscillated between orange and inky black, as if noting time for some ancient tune no longer sung or heard. A few sleepy birds started their early flight, skimming just above the water.

Turning, he saw a full moon descend above

the castle in the distance. Though its glory threatened to vanish with the day, it shone brilliant and yellow, the dark sky now a navy blue punctuated by a few remaining bright stars. Dark blue water rippled beneath it as the silvery rays danced on the surface. The sleeping palace lay beyond, barely visible through the wintry branches.

"It is mine by right, and I share it with whomever I please." And thus saying she placed her arm over his neck. A wind blew, and her long hair completely covered the royal cloak on his back. "I will share it with you," she said looking at him. "That is my promise to you." It was then that she described the conditions of his acceptance into her kingdom.

He needed to perform three difficult feats, all while being covered by the woolen cloak. First, he must stay awake all night during the full moon. Next, he must plunge into the magic pool—while fast asleep! After that he must awaken in the arms of dawn, being free and yet bound!

With this new knowledge, the unicorn became more determined to rid himself of his spots. Each month he waited for the full moon and he tried to stay awake. He could not stay awake, even for one hour. Even so, each morning, the princess welcomed him back for a new day of enjoyment together.

And each day as they re-entered the courtyard at twilight, in obedience to the king, the unicorn cringed at the gate. There hung the reminder that he was not a white unicorn. No red ribbon streamed from his neck. Rubbing his nose in the soft wool of the cloak, he reminded himself of the princess's love.

As the years passed, the princess matured. The floating curls of her youth grew to cataracts of gossamer hair. She grew tall and graceful, beautiful in manner and appearance. But the unicorn stayed small. His spots looked dowdier than ever, and even the once white hair began to sallow. Still, the princess left her lamp out for him each evening and faithfully lent him her wool cloak, day and night.

Years passed. At least a hundred years passed. The princess's white hair reached from the crown of her magnificent head all the way to her lovely feet. It shone like sunlight on a blanket of fresh snow. Her countenance became alabaster and fair, having no wrinkle or blemish. Her features, instead of diminishing with age, had matured with wisdom and the beauty that comes from a long life of loving and doing good. She had done both very well. Especially, she had loved and done good for her spotted little unicorn.

It was at that time, the same time of year when they had first found the unicorn, that her father indicated to her that it was now *time*.

It happened on the evening of a full moon.

The sky had just cleared after a day of heavy snow. The unicorn began to leave the palace to attempt the futile vigil. Foolishly, he thought to succeed in the three feats and thus surprise the princess in the morning with his new white coat. But on this night the princess pulled the cloak right off his back, saying he could not have it!

What could this mean? Did she no longer want him? Was this the fate of unicorns? When their princesses grew old would they discard their pets? But surely—surely, oh, those wretched spots!

She fixed on him a dark gaze. "Many long years you have been a guest in my father's house." Her voice was terrible. "But you cannot live here. This is the Castle of the White Unicorn. You are a unicorn with spots. Have you ever tried to rid yourself of those spots?"

He bowed his head until his horn rested on the ground. She knew he had tried. His legs could scarcely bear the weight of his own discolored body.

"Have you?"

"I cannot," his voice barely audible.

"True, so I must make a way for you. Then you may return to my house and to me forever."

The unicorn looked up expectantly.

"You must first go outside into the moonlight without the cloak."

"But I would never!"

"Then," she said, "you must fall asleep."

"I mustn't!" he wailed.

"*Can* you stay awake?"

"Nooooo."

"And while you are sleeping, you will plunge into the pool." She spoke as if to clarify difficult instructions. And yet it made no sense. The thought of the pool caused his limbs to tremble.

"Then, you must wake up at the first light of dawn, being bound and yet free!"

"Oh! Oh! Oh! These are means of undoing me! It's all wrong! If I stand in the light with no cloak, I fail. If I sleep in the light of the moon,

I fail. If I fall in the water while asleep, I drown. If I wake up at the first light of dawn, I have already failed to stay awake. And if I am bound, how can I be free?"

"Will you do this for me?"

"Do this for you?" the unicorn asked. "I cannot do it for myself. Moreover, I cannot will myself to die!"

"Then I must do it for you. Come with me." She dropped the cloak to the floor, left the palace, and went out into the night. He stared at the cloak with longing, but followed her. In the courtyard, he stopped.

The unicorn had never known the princess to go outdoors at night, save the time she rescued him from the pool. Now she strode out, straight toward her pond. He dared not step into the moonlight.

"Come, my love," she called again almost carelessly. He took a step.

She lay down by the edge of the pool as she had next to her father years before. Gently, she blew on the water. The unicorn felt the hair stand up on his back as a gentle breeze caught him from behind. Fear anchored his feet. She blew again, only this time harder.

An unexpected blast of wind blew the unicorn off balance. He stumbled forward into the light of the moon.

"There, you see. You've come out into the moon without the wool."

The mere thought of it shot through the

unicorn like a jolt, and he staggered.

"Here." She stood next to him tall, like an ancient snow-covered mountain. "I'll touch you, and you'll feel better."

The moment she touched him, his legs strengthened. He felt strong, like a weaned foal.

"And now you will fall asleep."

"Oh, but I do not want to." He lowered his head in shame.

"And why not?" Her eyebrows rose.

"I am afraid, because I can never stay awake, but I am supposed to . . . but I can't, even when I want to." He hated the sound of his own voice. "I have tried."

The air was filled with the musical sounds of her laughter. "That fear is not from me." She cradled his head and rubbed his muzzle with her hair.

The princess began to sing. This song he had never heard; yet it seemed he already knew the words. The tune sounded ancient and chanting, yet the words were fresh like air made sweet by rain. She sang of knowledge mixed together with innocence. She sang of things that were the same, and things that were opposite.

As her voice crooned softly, she stroked his mane. His heart calmed as it had the first night when she fed him rose petals. It didn't matter. This was all that mattered. There he was, helpless in her arms and covered with spots. And she cared for him anyway. He would do anything to stay with her. No matter what she asked of him. He might even be willing to die.

"But oh, to die!" he thought.

She kissed him. Fears abated. He drifted off to sleep.

The princess lay the unicorn on the frozen ground, his sides rising and lowering rhythmically as he slept. This was no ordinary sleep. It was like the sleep a child sleeps before being born into the world, a gift to be granted and granted only by one in whose veins royal blood courses.

The princess stood to begin her work. In the silvery light her body began to sway. She danced, slowly, swinging her arms back and forth. The solemn evergreen that had stood as a sentinel over the magic pool began to sway. The wind stirred. The pool rippled and gurgled as some underground force agitated it. The wind rose and whirlwinds of snow exploded around the feet of the ancient woman. Her hair twisted skyward upward into the sky.

As the wind lifted her hair, her fingers flew to work. She gathered three handfuls of hair and braided the strands into a cord the size of a small rope.

She tied a loop in the end, and lowered it like a wreath over the neck of the sleeping beast. The moon approached its zenith. She hadn't much time.

Kneeling, she began, strand-by-strand to reclaim her hair from the high wind and tuck the strands around the beast. Hoary blasts of wind stung her face and hands. Grasping each lock of hair, she wove it around her darling pet, covering him in a cocoon. The wind could not harm him now, nor the snow, nor the probing rays of the moon, nor the waters of her pool, nor even the deadly powers which resided in it.

When she was satisfied, she stood and lifted him in her arms. Drawing a deep breath, she breathed into the cocoon. And with one final breath, she plunged into the chilling waters. Down she went.

Down past the soft warmth of the snow and the coolness of the moon's light. Away from the clapping praise of the trees. Away from the storm. Away from life. Away from home. Away from the servants, her constant companions from her youth. Away from the beloved king whom she had obeyed her whole life long. Away from the fresh rising of the sun. Away from the hope of anything that is glorious, warm, or beautiful, or good.

The eye of the moon seemed determined

not to lose sight of her, its light dancing on the surface of the pool. The moon, obeying the laws to which it was subject, began its long descent to the horizon. The princess drifted down in the chilling darkness.

The water grew thick from the cold. Her arms ached. The farther she drifted, the closer she came to the danger of which she had once warned the unicorn. She sensed it hiding in the crevices of the dark pool. She braced herself for the attack.

Silently, the snakes leapt into action. Their red

bodies moved like bloody ribbons. They lunged at the cargo wound tightly within the princess's hair. But each strike aimed at the bundle missed its mark and hit the princess instead, shredding her sleeves and tearing at her flesh. The icy waters of the pool ran red with the life in her veins. Wound after wound bled, staining her beautiful snow-white hair all the way through to her tiny bundle. The snakes withdrew in silent victory.

The princess summoned the last of her strength. Knowing she had not much time, she tore a tiny hole in the cocoon. The last few bubbles of air drifted up, and she, with great effort, breathed into it the last of her breath. Pressing the hole against her, she locked her arms around the sleeping beast.

In silence she drifted. As darkness and cold claimed her last full measure of love, she waited. All that was left lay in the waiting.

At the breaking of the new day, a light glistened on the surface of the water. Lifting her face, the princess saw her father looking down into the pool and heard him say, "Come up, my daughter, and bring forth the dawn, the new dawn."

The princess began to rise. The waters were illumined, not only by the early rays of the sun, but by her own brilliant countenance. Her tattered clothing sank away, revealing a sleeveless blue gown. Only the cocoon and the braided strand, once stained with her blood, remained white. Rising with her wooly cocoon, she passed the snakes sleeping in their crevices. At her brightness, they blanched from red to white, and then charred to black, impotent worms.

Each moment she rose, her hair regained it former color, once again reflecting the radiance of the sun.

Above she could see the face of her father smiling. All the servants stood with him. As they rose out of the pool, the servants gasped. The princess was young again!

Nature came to life. It both lightly snowed and rained, though there was not a cloud in the sky. Birds swooped and twittered. The needles on the great pine tree danced.

The princess knelt. With a wave of her finger, nature quieted. The servants gathered as she prepared to tear open the cocoon.

The king nodded and the princess tore away the wrap. There was a long pause. A somewhat confused unicorn untucked his nose from under his hind leg. He blinked great, wondering eyes and rose to his feet. With a shake the remaining wrap fell to the ground. Around his neck hung the silver braid of hair with which the princess had bound him. A stunned silence fell on the servants. There stood a beautiful white unicorn with a silver braid hanging to the ground. Bound, and yet free. Having been covered in the light of the moon by her hair. Asleep, and having awakened in the arms of dawn, the very dawn of dawns: the princess herself.

Into the palace they went, a jubilant procession led by the king, beside the dazed unicorn in the arms of the princess. She carried him over the threshold, and into the palace where she deposited him on the floor. The servants cheered! The unicorn startled. Craning his neck, he turned to see his body. Pure white! He picked up and examined each foot. They were as pink as lamb's ears! "My horn?" he asked, trying to look up.

"White as a pearl," the princess said.

She lifted off the silver braid. Her father replaced it with a ribbon, red of course.

The king held a great feast to honor the princess and her unicorn and all the servants attended as guests.

From that day forward, the unicorn gained freedom to go wherever he pleased, day or night, without the wool cloak. Yet, in his new freedom, he will not leave the princess. Some say the ribbon binds him. Others say it is her hair, which once bound him. Yet, I have seen the two of them together, and I am sure that what binds him is much more than ribbons or hair!

www.ingramcontent.com/pod-product-compliance
Lightning Source LLC
LaVergne TN
LVHW021743060526
838200LV00052B/3447